DATE DUE

9/86	11/5		

All night long, the light is on in Mr. Bohm's window.
From the street, you can see him pacing up and down,
back and forth, pondering.

When he gets home to his room, deep wrinkles appear on his forehead.
If a herring begins its life in the water but then gets used to living on land,
can it still swim, or...?

Mr. Bohm walks slowly home, and you can tell he is thinking about something very important. Can a herring drown, he wonders, or did it remember it was a herring when it landed in the cold water?

He looks at his watch. He waits for a long time. But the herring is gone.

Mr. Bohm throws himself down on the pier. He sees the rings in the water grow wider and wider. He waits...

All of a sudden the herring has disappeared!

Mr. Bohm is deep in thought. He doesn't notice there's a hole in the pier.

that birds have wings and can fly, while the rest of us are forced to walk?

Why is it, Mr. Bohm wonders...

It has gotten so used to its dry life that it even avoids puddles in the street.

Today I'll show the herring the ocean, Mr. Bohm decides.

The talented herring gets more and more habits that are unusual for a fish.

At first, Mr. Bohm just walks back and forth in front of the house, but soon the herring is able to accompany him on his long walks.

The herring makes rapid progress, and before long, it is following Mr. Bohm around. In no time, it has grown so used to Mr. Bohm that it becomes sad when he has to leave the house.

By now, the herring is moving around with such ease that Mr. Bohm decides to take it along on his walks. He makes a leash and carefully attaches it behind the herring's gills.

Now we need to find a way for the
herring to get around, thinks Mr.
Bohm. He shows it how to lift its
head, how to crawl like a snake, and
how to use its fins. Mr. Bohm
practices with the herring every
morning.

One morning, Mr. Bohm takes the herring out of the aquarium. He carefully sets it down on the floor.

Finally, Mr. Bohm removes the last of the water. It seems to him that the herring looks happy as it flops around on the wet sand. I can't let the herring get too dry, thinks Mr. Bohm. He waters it every day.

Gradually Mr. Bohm begins to reduce the amount of water in the tank.
Every day, he takes out a bit more. Soon there are only a couple of inches left.
The herring gets used to splashing along on the bottom of the aquarium.

When Mr. Bohm gets home, he prepares his aquarium. First he puts a little sand on the bottom, and then he fills it up with water. He drops the herring in. Mr. Bohm thinks it looks surprised, but soon it's swimming around calmly. I'll have to go slowly, Mr. Bohm thinks. The herring has to get comfortable in its new surroundings before I take the next step.

Suddenly he catches a herring!

The more he thinks about it, the more certain he becomes that if a fish just got the right training, it could learn to live on land.

Early the next morning, Mr. Bohm heads for the ocean.

When he gets home to his room, deep wrinkles appear on his forehead.
Could it be that fish live in the water out of habit? What if you gradually got a fish
used to it – could it learn to live on land?
All night long, the light is on in Mr. Bohm's window.

Mr. Bohm walks home, and you can tell he is thinking about something very important. Why is it, he wonders, that fish can't live on land?

The fish flop around on the pier. They don't like it, thinks Mr. Bohm. They don't like coming up into the air.

Mr. Bohm watches the boys fishing in the harbor. He sees them catch one fish, and then another.

Mr. Bohm inspects the fish in the market. He looks at the dead pikes and the wriggling eels.

Mr. Bohm sees an aquarium in a pet store. He studies how easily the fish move in the water.

Why is it, thinks Mr. Bohm, that the dog chose that particular tree? Nothing is too big or too small to escape Mr. Bohm's notice.

On his daily walks he always comes across something that requires investigation.

Mr. Bohm, who is a thoughtful person, often ponders the mysteries of life. When he does, deep wrinkles appear on his forehead, and he barely notices the world around him. Why is it, he might ask himself, that birds have wings and can fly, while the rest of us are forced to walk? Why is it that people wear clothes but other creatures go around stark naked? These are the kinds of problems Mr. Bohm likes to consider.

This book is dedicated to Alphonse Allais (1850–1905),
one of whose anecdotes inspired
the telling of this tale

E green

Rabén & Sjögren Stockholm
Translation copyright © 1992 by Richard E. Fisher
All rights reserved
Pictures copyright © 1991 by Olof Landström
Originally published in Sweden by Rabén & Sjögren
under the title *Herr Bohm och sillen*, text copyright © 1991 by Peter Cohen
Library of Congress catalog card number: 91-42054
Printed in Denmark
First edition, 1992
ISBN 91 29 62056 2

MR. BOHM AND THE HERRING

Peter Cohen
Pictures by Olof Landström

TRANSLATED BY RICHARD E. FISHER

R&S
BOOKS

Stockholm   New York   London   Adelaide   Toronto